Dear Parent:

Your child's love of reading starts here!

Every child learns to read in a different way and at his or her own speed. Some go back and forth between reading levels and read favorite books again and again. Others read through each level in order. You can help your young reader improve and become more confident by encouraging his or her own interests and abilities. From books your child reads with you to the first books he or she reads alone, there are I Can Read Books for every stage of reading:

SHARED READING
Basic language, word repetition, and whimsical illustrations, ideal for sharing with your emergent reader

BEGINNING READING
Short sentences, familiar words, and simple concepts for children eager to read on their own

READING WITH HELP
Engaging stories, longer sentences, and language play for developing readers

READING ALONE
Complex plots, challenging vocabulary, and high-interest topics for the independent reader

I Can Read Books have introduced children to the joy of reading since 1957. Featuring award-winning authors and illustrators and a fabulous cast of beloved characters, I Can Read Books set the standard for beginning readers.

A lifetime of discovery begins with the magical words **"I Can Read!"**

Visit www.icanread.com for information
on enriching your child's reading experience.

I Can Read® and I Can Read Book® are trademarks of HarperCollins Publishers.

The Angry Birds Movie 2: Best Enemies
Based on the screenplay written by Peter Ackerman
©2019 Rovio Entertainment Corporation and Rovio Animation Ltd. Rovio, Angry Birds, Bad Piggies, Mighty Eagle and all related properties, titles, logos and characters are trademarks of Rovio Entertainment Corporation and Rovio Animation Ltd. and are used with permission. The Angry Birds Movie 2 ©2019 Columbia Pictures Industries, Inc. All Rights Reserved. Printed in the United States of America. No part of this book may be used or reproduced in any manner whatsoever without written permission except in the case of brief quotations embodied in critical articles and reviews. For information address HarperCollins Children's Books, a division of HarperCollins Publishers, 195 Broadway, New York, NY 10007.
www.icanread.com

Library of Congress Control Number: 2019936833
ISBN 978-0-06-294537-2

Book design by Brenda Angelilli
19 20 21 22 23 LSCC 10 9 8 7 6 5 4 3 2 1 ❖ First Edition

2
READING WITH HELP

I Can Read!

THE ANGRY BIRDS 2 MOVIE

BEST ENEMIES
adapted by Tomas Palacios

HARPER
An Imprint of HarperCollinsPublishers

Hi, everyone, it's me again.

Your old friend Red.

I'm still angry.

I'm still a bird.

I'm also a hero!

Remember Leonard?

He is leader of the pigs

on Piggy Island.

The pigs are our enemies.

They tried to eat our eggs!

I helped save the eggs and the day.

Being a hero is a big job.

I keep all of Bird Island safe.

I protect my fellow birds.

I especially protect the hatchlings.

They are quite the handful!

These days,

the pigs don't steal our eggs.

Now we just play pranks

on each other.

The pigs once dropped crabs on us!

Everyone ran for cover.

Luckily, no one was hurt,

but it was annoying!

One day, Leonard knocked on my door,

asking for a truce.

I thought he came to play a prank,

so I tied him up.

But he didn't come to play a prank.

"We've discovered a third island.

Eagle Island!

The eagles are plotting

to destroy us all!" he said.

Leonard told me about an eagle named Zeta.

Zeta was from Eagle Island.

She had a volcanic superweapon.

It was so powerful it could destroy both Piggy and Bird Islands!

I untied Leonard.

"This is bigger than pranks,"
Leonard said.

I knew he was right.

"Let's put aside our differences
and work together," Leonard said.

I couldn't let Bird Island
get destroyed.

I smiled at Leonard and said,
"What we really need . . . is a hero.
I'm in."

"Wonderful!" Leonard replied.
"We'll have to get a team together."

Leonard and I went to visit Bomb.

I knew Bomb would be perfect
for the team.

Bomb wasn't the smartest bird,
but he packed quite a boom!

Bomb could explode if under attack.

He was a perfect pick to fight Zeta!

Next, we visited the fastest bird
on Bird Island.
Chuck could think fast, talk fast,
and move even faster.
"This guy's so fast
he can beat time itself
in a footrace," I told Leonard.

"Hey, Chuck!" I yelled.

"We're putting together a team!"

"I think we're on it!" Bomb added.

Chuck zipped by so fast

we couldn't see him!

 "I'm in!" he yelled as he ran by.

Our third stop was

Mighty Eagle's mountain.

Mighty Eagle was a legend

around Bird Island.

He was the only bird that could fly.

"You've come to the right eagle,"

Mighty Eagle said.

He struck a brave pose.

Then he struck another pose.

And another pose. And another pose!

We had a good team so far.

We had speed and flight.

We had firepower and pigs.

But we needed smarts as well.

Chuck had an idea.

He said we should check out

Avian Academy.

This school is where the brightest

and best birds go to study.

Chuck told us about Silver,
his sister.
Silver skipped four grades
and was top of her class.

Silver was giving a presentation
on her new invention—Super String!
She was just what the team needed!
"I like her," said Leonard.
And just like that we had
the final member of our team!

We went to Mighty Eagle's cave.

Leonard put on his Pig Projector.

"Each of you has been selected

because you are the best

in your field," said Leonard.

It was now time to tell the group

our plan.

I showed the group our plan

on the Pig Projector.

First, travel from Bird Island

to Eagle Island.

Then climb all the way up

to the volcano.

Finally, stop Zeta's evil plan!

Leonard told us

about his top secret project.

It was a super-submarine.

The pigs built it

because they were good with gadgets.

The next day,

we boarded the submarine.

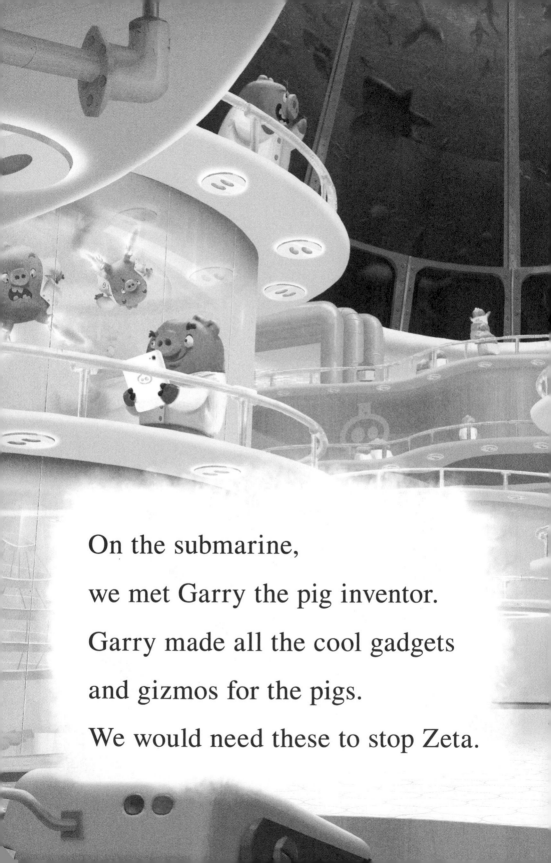

On the submarine,

we met Garry the pig inventor.

Garry made all the cool gadgets

and gizmos for the pigs.

We would need these to stop Zeta.

Our team was finally ready!
We arrived at Eagle Island.
The Super Pig Submarine
rose to the surface.
It broke through the ice.
The doors opened,
and we stepped out.

We had speed and flight.

We had firepower and pigs.

And we had smarts.

Most of all, we had each other.

This super-team was ready

to save the day!